FOR AYURVEDA, SKINCARE & FMCG STARTUPS

Rishabh's strategic thinking sets him apart. Turning complex marketing challenges into actionable plans that deliver results is his superpower.

GURPREET BHATIA, *Founder & CEO, Flying Saints. The UX/UI King*

The
Ayurveda
Giant's

1-PAGE

MARKETING
SUCCESS PLAN

The Ayurveda Giant's

1-PAGE MARKETING SUCCESS PLAN

RISHABH GUPTA

Worldwide Published by
Pendown Press

PENDOWN PRESS

An ISO 9001 & ISO 14001 Certified Co.,

Regd. Office: 2525/193, 1st Floor, Onkar Nagar-A, Tri Nagar, Delhi-110035

Ph.: 09350849407, 09312235086

E-mail: info@pendownpress.com

Branch Office: 1A/2A, 20, Hari Sadan, Ansari Road, Daryaganj, New Delhi-110002

Ph.: 011-45794768

Website: PendownPress.com

First Edition: 2023

ISBN: 978-93-5554-568-8

Layout and Cover Designed by Pendown Graphics Team

Printed and Bound in India by Thomson Press India Ltd.

Contents

Quote i

Dedication of Book ii

Disclaimer iii

What People Say About Rishabh iv

Acknowledgements vi

My Sincere Gratitude viii

Pinky Promise After Reading This Book ix

Who Should Read This Book x

Your 1st Step To Enter The World of Marketing

Chapter 1

Developing A Marketing Mindset 1

Chapter 2

Marketing 7

– What is Customer Touchpoint?

– The Right Sequence

Chapter 3

Choosing Your Audience 11

Chapter 4

Own Your Niche 17

Chapter 5

Content Creation For Building Authority   23

Chapter 6

Create Content That Converts   26

What Will You Choose?   30

Choose The Right Person For Building
The Marketing Dominated Company   31

About The Author   34

Book Summary   36

Quote

"Nothing gets transformed in your life until your mind is transformed."

~Ifeanyi Enoch Onuoha

Dedication of Book

This book is dedicated to two incredible women who have profoundly shaped my life. The first is my biological mother, who unfortunately passed away in 2013. Her love, support, and guidance have been immeasurable, and I miss her dearly.

The second woman I want to honor is my wife's mother, who has become like a second mother to me. Her kindness, wisdom, and unwavering support have been a constant source of inspiration and strength. She truly is a remarkable soul, and I am immensely grateful for everything she has done for me.

I also want to express my heartfelt gratitude to my wife Supriya, whose unwavering support and love have been essential in bringing this book to fruition. Without her, this book would not have been possible.

And last but certainly not least, I want to extend a special shoutout to Sandali, my darling sister-in-law, who has always shown me love and support, even when I was just her jiju (brother-in-law). Her presence in my life has been a true blessing.

To my biological mother, my second mother, my wife, and my sister-in-law - thank you for being the remarkable women that you are. This book is dedicated to each of you.

Disclaimer

The information presented in this book is based on my personal experiences and practical methods, and it aims to provide general guidance. I have taken every measure to ensure the accuracy and comprehensiveness of the information provided. However, I do not make any, warranties or guarantees, whether expressed or implied, about the completeness, accuracy, reliability, suitability or availability with respect to the information contained in this book. I will not be liable for any loss or damage, including without limitation indirect or consequential loss or damage, or any loss or damage whatsoever arising from loss of data or profits arising out of, or in connection with, the use of this book. Any reliance you place on such information is therefore strictly at your own risk.

What People Say About Rishabh

1. One word for Rishabh – The New Future Of Marketing....

   ~Sachin Chaturvedi,
   Director Of A Leather Factory

2. Rishabh=Marketing...Period.....

   ~Sankalp Bansal,
   CEO & Founder Vidvox Consultancy

3. I have known Rishabh since last 6 months only and the way he has a grip over marketing principles is simply amazing. Whenever I talk to him he always gives me lot of transforming information that makes me think that we unnecessary cry for competition, there is no competition in the market. You can stand out in the market if you change beliefs and think with a bigger picture.

   ~Himanshu Chadha,
   Exec. Director Aryanveda

4. Rishabh is a true leader in the marketing space. His ability to inspire and motivate his team has led to a culture of creativity and innovation, and his dedication to delivering exceptional results is second to none.

   ~Swapnil Sharma,
   VP Sales, BUSINESSNEXT

5. Rishabh's strategic thinking is what sets him apart. He's able to take complex marketing challenges and turn them into actionable plans that deliver results. His ability to think outside the box is a true asset to our team.

    ~Gurpreet Bhatia,
    Founder & CEO Flying Saints.
    The UX/UI King

6. Rishabh's attention to detail is unparalleled. He's always looking for ways to improve campaigns, and his deep understanding of customer behavior has led to some incredibly successful marketing initiatives.

    ~Shaista Pathan,
    CEO/Founder Skin Reiaya,
    Luxury Ethical Skincare Based out in London

7. Rishabh is an exceptional marketer with a profound understanding of the field. His expertise and strategic approach have greatly benefited our business, leading to remarkable growth and success.

    ~Atul Modi,
    Director, AXL World

Acknowledgements

Acknowledgements serve as a means of expressing gratitude to those who have contributed to the creation of a book. In my case, I would like to extend my heartfelt thanks to the numerous authors whose works have inspired me, and the many individuals who have supported me on my journey of discovery.

As I wrote this book, I realized that the content was not entirely new. Rather, it was the result of my readings and learnings from my mentors, various authors and my own experiments. I firmly believe that instead of attempting to invent something entirely new, it is better to model those techniques that have been tried and tested and are known to be evergreen strategies.

In the words of the great artist, Pablo Picasso, "Good artists copy, great artists steal." I have followed this philosophy in my work, and I have discovered that it has helped me in learning from the finest and enhancing my own skills. I have learned from the greats, and I have taken their ideas and made them my own.

I want to thank all the authors whose work I have studied throughout the years. Their words have inspired me, and their knowledge has played a vital role in the creation of this book. I have learned from you and I have incorporated your ideas into my work.

I also want to thank my friends and family who have supported me throughout my journey. Their encouragement and belief in me have helped me to persevere through the challenges that come with writing a book. Thank you for your constant love and support.

Lastly, I want to express my gratitude to my readers. It is your interest in this book that has made it all possible. I hope that the knowledge and insights shared within these pages will prove invaluable to you, and that you will find the strategies presented here to be useful in your own life.

In conclusion, I want to express my sincere gratitude to all the people who have contributed to the creation of this book. I hope that it will inspire others to learn from the greats and to incorporate their ideas into their own work. Thank you all, and I wish you all the best on your personal journeys of discovery.

I am thankful to My Friend Dinesh Verma, CEO, Pendown Press and his team for their support and suggestions throughout the creative process.

My Sincere Gratitude

- Mr Akshar Yadav, Chairman, CEO & International Marketing Strategist, who is a true inspiration for me and pushed me ssuuupppeeer haaarrdd to implement the marketing principles he taught me.

- Mr. Gupreet Bhatia, CEO & Founder Flying Saints Who Connected & Referred Me To The USE & GO Community.

- My USE (Ultimate Sales Engine)
  & GO (Get Overbooked) Tribe

- All the captains of USE (Ultimate Sales Engine)
  & GO (Get Overbooked) Tribe

- Sanjiv Ranjan Ji (Guruji): Manifestation, I always thought is just a word, but the true meaning & application of manifestation is taught by him. With the help of manifestation is the reason I have been able to write this book. He taught me that manifestation only works when you take small actions and break your intent/wishes in parts.

- Dinesh Verma, Director of Pendown Press that made it possible to launch this book.

Pinky Promise
After Reading This Book

As you approach the conclusion of this book, I want to make a big promise to you - that you will emerge with a renewed sense of inspiration and empowerment. You will have gained valuable knowledge and practical tools that you can apply to your life to help you achieve your goals and aspirations. The insights and strategies you've acquired will stay with you long after you turn the last page, and I am confident that you will be able to use them to create a brighter future for yourself and those around you.

- **Big promise:** To help readers become a great marketer

- **Know the big picture:** Understand the overall landscape of marketing

- **Expand your viewpoint:** Think beyond traditional marketing approaches

- **Know what is marketing:** Learn the core concepts and principles of marketing

- **Develop a marketing mindset:** Adopt a strategic and creative approach to marketing

- **Hardcore implementation:** Take action and apply the concepts learned in real-world situations

- **Become a great marketer:** Continuously improve and refine marketing skills to achieve success

Who Should Read This Book

1. **Early stage startups in the field of Ayurveda:** This book provides valuable insights, strategies, and practical advice that are specifically tailored to entrepreneurs and businesses in the Ayurveda industry.

2. **FMCG (Fast-Moving Consumer Goods) and skincare marketers:** Professionals working in FMCG and skincare industries can benefit from this book as it offers relevant guidance on branding, market positioning, consumer behavior, product differentiation, and effective marketing strategies within these sectors. It aims to help marketers in gaining a competitive edge and effectively promoting their FMCG or skincare products to the target audience.

3. **Founders and CEOs:** The book also caters to founders and CEOs of startups operating in the Ayurveda, FMCG, and skincare industries. The book's objective is to equip leaders with the knowledge and tools necessary for growth and sustainability.

Overall, this book caters to early stage startups in Ayurveda, FMCG and skincare marketers, as well as founders and CEOs seeking to enhance their understanding and expertise in these domains.

I intend for this book to serve as a practical and commonsense guide that helps you define and become a great marketer. It is designed for anyone who is interested in adding value to their organization. I hope it will be illuminating and fun, enlivened by my irreverent spirit that has helped and hindered my career in equal measure.

Why Ayurveda Marketing & What Got Me Hooked

Ayurveda, the ancient Indian system of natural medicine, captured my attention with its profound wisdom and holistic approach to health. Its ability to help people live healthy and fulfilling lives resonated deeply with me. When i joined the World's Leading Ayurvedic Brand that does the 360 degree business on Ayurveda "Kairali Ayurvedic Group", as a marketer, I recognized the immense potential of Ayurveda in the global market and way it can heal and help you live a healthy lifestyle. In fact Ayurvedic therapies, Ayurvedic medicines & Ayurvedic cosmetics when i used i saw amazing benefits on my health & well being. These positive outcomes really hooked me and I decided that I will market Ayurveda and promote a healthy natural lifestyle to everyone and do my best within Kairali Ayurvedic Group to spread Ayurveda across the globe through my marketing strategies & tactics. Various age-old brands and the new entrants in Ayurveda also got very aggressive in their marketing during the covid era. The opportunity to promote products that not only enhance physical well-being but also connect individuals with nature was irresistible.

Currently serving as the Vice President of Marketing for the renowned Kairali Ayurvedic Group, I am thrilled to apply my knowledge and skills to propagate Ayurveda worldwide. The remarkable impact and positive response from our audience affirm that our efforts are making a difference in people's lives.

Your 1st Step
To Enter
The World of Marketing

Chapter 1

Developing A Marketing Mindset

"When You Believe,
Your Mind Will Find The Way."
~David J. Schwantz
Author of "The Magic Of Thinking Big"

In the world of business, having a marketing mindset is vital for success. It's not just about selling products or services; it requires self-belief that you can excel as a marketer and focus on asking relevant questions on how to become a great marketer and what actions should I take to become a great marketer. Developing a marketing mindset requires a shift in perspective and being open to new ideas and opportunities. In this chapter, we will explore the key elements of a marketing mindset and how they can drive business growth and financial success.

1. **Think Big & Start Believing In Yourself:** A marketing mindset demands that, it is essential to think beyond the limitations of your current circumstances. This involves envisioning the possibilities and setting audacious goals. Don't limit yourself with self-doubt or negative beliefs. Instead, focus on the potential for achieving greatness and the impact you can have in your

industry. When your inner self is strong then only you will be able to make the external environment strong.

2. **See the bigger picture:** You have to eliminate any false ideas you may have on a subject, and this can only happen by installing the "mantras" & "sutras" of the timeless marketing principles. Do deep research on how brands are prioritizing marketing over product sales. iPhone is not the best phone in the world but still people line up and aspire to buy the phone, not because of the phone but the way they do marketing. Starbucks coffee is not the best coffee in the world but still consumers line up to their stores and spend money on one of the most expensive coffee just because of their marketing. So when you start seeing the bigger picture all limitations and competitions will be deleted.

3. **Expand your viewpoint:** Be free from narrow thinking and explore different perspectives. Embrace diversity of thought and seek out fresh ideas from various sources. This open-mindedness will allow you to discover innovative marketing strategies and adapt to changing consumer preferences. Lot of us think that sales generate revenue, it's important to expand your viewpoint and recognize that **"Sales Is The Manifestation Of Right Marketing"** Marketing Drives Income, If you focus on only sales your product becomes a commodity and you have to sell at loss or play a discount game and just play a survival game, but if you focus on marketing, you move away from

commoditized market and build a brand where customers pay at your own price. **Just Think About The Brands You Use, Wear & Consume.**

4. **Break free from limiting beliefs:** Don't let self-imposed limitations hold you back. Sales may seem challenging, but you can thrive with the appropriate mindset and abilities. Remember, marketing is not just the responsibility of a specific role or department. It's a fundamental element of every business, and with practice, anyone can become an effective marketer. **Marketing Is Everything** and **Everything Is Marketing.**

5. **Big viewpoint, big money:** A marketing mindset means understanding that expanding your reach and impact can lead to higher profits. By thinking ambitiously and executing strategic marketing initiatives, you can attract more customers, boost sales, and ultimately, achieve financial success.

6. **Embrace a warrior mentality:** Adopt a fearless and determined approach to business. A marketing mindset requires perseverance, flexibility, and a willingness to take calculated risks. Treat every challenge as an opportunity to learn and grow, and don't shy away from competition. Embrace the mindset of a warrior, ready to conquer obstacles and achieve triumph.

Developing a marketing mindset is an ongoing process that necessitates continuous learning, experimentation, and adaptation. By thinking big, seeing the bigger picture, expanding your viewpoint, overcoming limiting beliefs, and embracing a warrior mentality, you can unlock your full potential as a marketer and propel your business towards unparalleled success. **Remember, success in business is not just about what you sell; it's about how effectively you market it.**

My Story When I Had A Limied Viewpoint

I always used to think that I am not a good marketer, I cannot do sales nor become a good salesperson. I can never become an author. Despite having so much experience in the industry, I was still the same old marketer. I have been continuously learning and reading books and courses, but I have never expanded my viewpoint nor implemented it

My Story When I Expanded My View Point

The book you currently hold in your hands is the result of my expanded view point and thinking big. When I started thinking that I am the best author on marketing I started learning, researching & implementing those learnings. I started manifesting myself that I am the finest marketer in the world. With manifestation, you need to take action, so I started taking action and broke down my goals in fractions, and started achieving them. I started experimenting with various marketing principles without fear of what anyone would say, I became fearless in implementing, I actively engaged with my customers, started speaking confidently in public and shared many invaluable marketing principles.

"From a day dreamer I became an action player"

Exercise

1. Take a moment to ponder for just 5 minutes about instances where your limited viewpoint hindered or delayed your progress like you said you don't have enough money to start your own business or run a marketing campaign because of no funds or you thought that it is cut throat market competition. These limited perspectives acted as barriers to taking action. Pull out a paper or notebook and write them down.

2. Begin expanding your viewpoint and refrain from being judgmental about what others say or you say, Embrace a learner's mindset and focus on how you can enhance yourself to become a great marketer. List down the pointers that come to your mind. For Example: I will become a great marketer, I am a great salesman, I actively seek solutions to become a better learner.

3. Start implementing and experimenting your ideas fearlessly. Remember, NOBODY CARES what you do, neither you should care what others say. Experiment & Learn and you will witness the transformative changes in yourself.

> *If you want to have a rising graph then*
> *you have to be a great marketer.*

Shift In View Point <Will Shift Your
Behavior <Will Give You New Actions
<Will Give You New Results.

Exercise

Your Limited View Point

- ....
- ....
- ....
- ....
- ....

Your Expanded View Point

- ....
- ....
- ....
- ....
- ....

List Down What Steps You Will Take To Become A Great Marketer

- ....
- ....
- ....
- ....
- ....

Chapter 2

Marketing

What is Marketing and What is NOT Marketing

We all are living in this myth that

- Marketing is an expense
- Marketing is a cost
- Marketing is digital marketing
- Marketing is advertising
- Marketing is sales
- Marketing comes after sales
- Marketing is a one time activity
- Marketing is Facebook or Google marketing
- Marketing is SEO and many more

I must tell you that THIS IS NOT MARKETING, These are just the resources, channels, sources & mediums of marketing.

Marketing Is

1. It is a game of winning Yesses and presenting your products in such a way that the potential customers come to you & is eager to buy.

2. Marketing Is All About Serving The Customer Needs.

Your every customer touchpoint should speak YES and convinces the customer to connect with you.

What is Customer Touchpoint?

The places or situations where your customer interacts with you includes Facebook, Google, Product Packaging, Marketing Collaterals, eBooks, Case Studies, Website, Sales Person, Social Media, ADs, and promos.

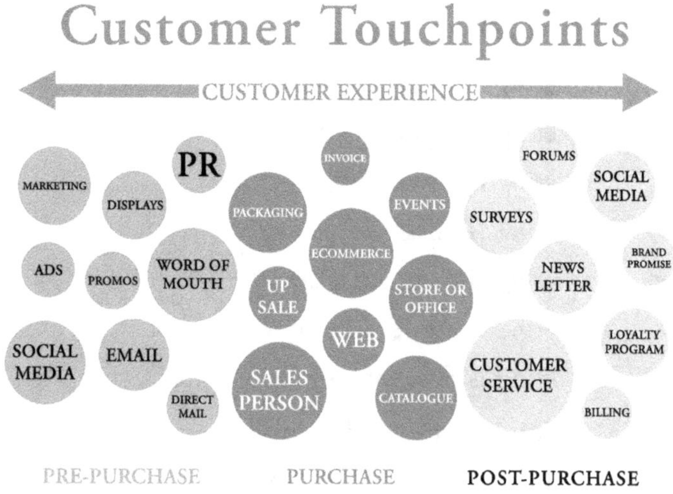

The Right Sequence

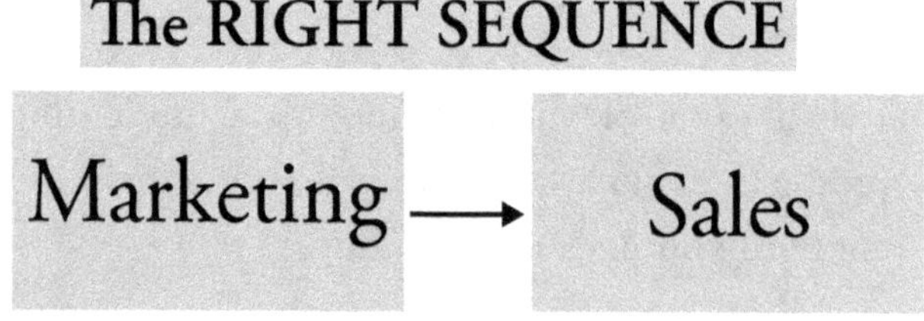

Exercise

Just take 5 min and think of the brands and their touchpoints where you got hooked like Apple, Starbucks, Amazon, Airtel, Jio, Mamaearth, Sugar Cosmetics, Dove, Dabur, Kama Ayurveda, Forest Essentials and many more.

For Selling anything you need to engage in MARKETING first.

Here is a simple and most jargon free definition of marketing.

If the circus is coming to the town and you paint a sign saying "Circus coming to your town on Saturday" that's **advertising.**

If you put a sign on the back of the elephant and walk it to town, that's **promotion.**

If the elephant walks through the minister's farmhouse and the local newspaper writes a story about it, that's **publicity.**

And if you get the minister to laugh about it, that's **public relations.**

If the town's citizens go to the circus, you show them entertainment booths, and explain how much fun they can have inside the circus and the booths, and you answer their questions, ultimately leading them to spend a lot at the circus. That's **sales.**

And if you planned the whole thing, that's marketing.

It is truly simple, Marketing is the strategy you use for getting your ideal audience to know, build trust, and create likability, ultimately converting them into your customers.

Without MARKETING, Nobody will know you exists.

Marketing is never the expense, it becomes expensive when you do WRONG marketing.

Chapter 3

Choosing Your Audience

In the highly competitive world of Ayurveda, skincare & FMCG, it is crucial to understand your ideal customer for the success of your brand. By Identifying and defining your target audience, you can customize your products, marketing strategies, and messaging to effectively meet their specific needs and desires. This chapter explores the process of defining the ideal customer for Ayurvedic, skincare & FMCG brands, empowering them to connect with their target market and nurture enduring customer relationships.

Step 1: Market Research

To define your ideal customer, the first step is to conduct comprehensive market research. This process includes gathering data and insights about your target market, such as demographics, psychographics, preferences, and purchasing behaviors. By talking to customers & analyzing existing customer data, conducting surveys, and studying market trends, you can identify patterns and common characteristics among your most loyal customers.

Demographics: Start by examining key demographic factors such as age, gender, location, and income level. This information forms the basis of understanding your target audience and empowers allows you to customize your product offerings and marketing messages accordingly. *For instance, younger customers may show greater interest in anti-aging and preventive skincare, while older customers might seek products that address specific concerns like wrinkles or pigmentation.*

Psychographics: Dive deeper into the psychographics of your ideal customer, aiming to understand their values, interests, lifestyles, and beliefs. *Consider their motivations for choosing Ayurvedic skincare products, whether it is a preference for natural ingredients, a desire for holistic wellness, or an interest in sustainability. This knowledge helps you align your brand messaging with their aspirations, enhancing the appeal and relatability of your products.*

Step 2: Creating Buyer Personas

Example of USER PERSONA: Ayurveda and Skin Care Buyer Persona.

Table 01: Demographics

Data Points	[MARKET] Answers
Name:	Neha Kapoor
Age:	35
Occupation:	Yoga Instructor
Annual Income:	Rs. 50,000
Marital Status:	Married
Family Situation:	Two children
Location:	Mumbai, India

Table 02: User Description
Neha Kapoor is a 35-year-old married Yoga Instructor with an annual income of Rs.50,000. She lives in Mumbai, India and has two children. Neha is health-conscious and values natural remedies. She seeks Ayurveda and skin care products that align with her lifestyle and promote holistic well-being.

Table 03: Psychographics

Data Points	[MARKET] Answers
Personal Characteristics:	Health-conscious, environmentally aware, prefers natural products, values traditional remedies
Hobbies:	Practicing yoga, meditation, reading books on holistic health, exploring nature
Interests:	Ayurveda, natural skincare, wellness retreats, sustainable living, herbal remedies
Personal Aspirations:	Maintaining a healthy lifestyle, achieving work-life balance, nurturing family relationships
Professional Goals:	Expanding her yoga practice, becoming a respected wellness influencer, creating online content to inspire others
Pains:	Lack of time for self-care, exposure to pollution, stress, skin concerns like acne or premature aging
Main Challenges:	Finding trusted Ayurveda and skin care brands, understanding product ingredients, balancing work and personal life effectively
Needs:	Effective and natural skincare solutions, holistic wellness guidance, reliable product recommendations, convenience in purchasing
Dreams:	Owning a wellness center, becoming a recognized authority in Ayurvedic practices, promoting sustainable and healthy living worldwide

Table 04: Shopping Behaviors

Data Points	[MARKET] Answers
Budget:	Moderate
Shopping Frequency:	Monthly
Preferred Channels:	Online stores, Ayurveda specialty shops, wellness centers
Online Behavior:	Researches product reviews and ingredients, seeks advice from online communities and social media
Search Terms:	Ayurvedic skincare, natural remedies for skin, organic beauty products
Preferred Brands:	Trusted Ayurveda brands, eco-friendly and sustainable skincare companies
Triggers	Positive customer reviews, recommendations from experts, promotional offers
Barriers:	Lack of product availability, high prices, skepticism towards new or unknown brands

Check reviews on amazon to see what people like and dislike, you can also check the website www.answerthepublic.com. Additionally, check Quora on what people are questioning the most.

Exercise

- Define your possible markets?

- Define your Audience?

    - Demographics: Age, gender, income level, geography, occupation, education, marital status, language, industry.

- Psychographics: lifestyle preferences, spending habits, hobbies, entertainment, vacation, reading, listening, watching habits.

Can you have more than 1 customer? YES, but focus on 1 Customer first who can give you the maximum business. The total addressable market has to be big enough to serve.

Rishabh's Ideal Customer: *Early stage startups in Ayurveda, FMCG, skincare businesses who want to grow their business from 0 to a billion dollar organization. My ideal customer should have a growth mindset, be marketing focused, visionary, open to trying new things, have clarity on what they want, and approach business with a collaborative approach. They want to create a differentiation in the market, they have a marketing mindset. This is just a snapshot of my buyer persona.*

CHECKS when defining your Ideal Customer?

1. If your customers will give you profits?

2. If your customers will give you repeat orders?

3. If your customers will refer you?

Profitable, Repeat & Refer is your ideal customer

You need to earn a minimum Profit margin of 25-50% with your ideal customer.

Repercussions of NOT having an ideal customer

- Your marketing message will not be clear
- No conversions
- Wastage of money in the wrong marketing
- Loss making customers
- Slow business growth
- Negative Brand Reputation

Chapter 4

Own Your Niche

Everything about marketing comes down to the audience—specifically, your target audience that we discussed in the previous chapter. Each business has a unique audience.. Once you successfully identify your audience, every marketing decision you make becomes easier because you can gather data to understand your audience better and you can begin building your service offerings and your marketing campaigns around their needs. More importantly, the narrower your focus, the better chance you have of standing out.

For example, sales professionals are often skilled at handling multiple tasks. It can be tempting to remain a generalist in order to try to secure as much work as possible.. When a potential client calls and asks for a product specialist sales person, the answer is always, "Yes, sure, we can do that!" Comparatively, a Cardiologist doctor is paid more than a general physician.

My niche is Marketing for Ayurveda, FMCG & Skin care startups only.

The Downsides of being a generalists

There are several potential downsides to saying yes to everything.

1. You can't possibly be an expert in all areas (unless you employ a large team of specialists in each area).

2. Your portfolio of work may appear unfocused. If you say yes to everything and then show photos of your wide variety of jobs to potential clients, they might think, "Gee, he does a lot, but I only see one example of a bathroom remodel. I wish I could see more examples. I wonder if he really has the right experience to do this job."

On the flip side, if you were to meet with a potential client who wanted her kitchen remodeled and you presented a portfolio of photos showcasing the many dazzling kitchens you have created, a bright light would shine around you. You would become the obvious authority in your field—a field that is quite crowded with generalists.

Benefits of Choosing a Niche

- Stand out against the competition, which are usually generalists.

- Increase appeal with your niche audience because they will feel confident they are working with an authority who understands their needs.

- Finding referral partners will be easier as you can collaborate with those who operate within your niche, plus those who focus on a complementary niche.

- You can establish yourself as the go-to choice for clients who need what you have to offer

- You may be able to raise your rates due to your specialty area of focus

How Your Business Can Thrive with a Niche Focus

When your business has a clearly defined niche, not only can you attract even more business from your ideal customers, you can also often command higher fees.

Examples of Potential Niches

Business	Niches
Face Serum:	Specifically, for professionals who face pollution from traveling through train or metros
Nutritionist:	Food allergies, weight loss, weight loss for women (or men), vegan living, gluten-free, diabetes:
Consultant:	Specific topic-focused, such as leadership for new managers, productivity for call centers, cultivating a remote workforce, launching new technologies
Holistic Doctor:	Allergies, menopause, sports injuries, pain management, fibromyalgia, smoking cessation
Hair oil:	For people who need hair growth & reduce hair fall
Moisturizing cream:	For men's only who want to reduce dark spots & pigmentation
Professional Speaker:	Sales strategies for women, leadership for government offices, team building for tech companies

Brands that are dominating with the niche

Brands	Their Niche
Avimee Herbals:	For Hair Growth & Hair Fall
Kairali Ayurvedic Products:	Ayurvedic oils for pain management focused on panchakarma centers
Traya Health:	For Hair Fall & Hair Growth
Mama earth:	Skincare products for babies & kids now they have expanded to other lines after dominating there niche
Cult Fit:	Fitness and health
Durmeric:	Liquified herbal extracts with a higher absorption rate and more potency
Nat Habit:	Freshly made, 100% natural beauty & wellness products inspired by ancient ayurvedic solutions.
Caffeine:	Coffee made skincare range
Sleepy Owl:	Cold Brew Coffees
Assembly:	Luggages & Travel Accessories for Ultra Travellers
Zappos:	Shoe Retailer
Wal Mart:	Everyday Low prices
Starbucks:	Coffee
Chaayos:	Chai
Canva.com:	Design platform for anyone who wants to design without any formal training.
Skin Reiaya:	Ethical Clean Beauty Skincare Range For Environment Stressors

How to Identify Your Niche Focus

Choosing the right path for your business is something that requires careful thought and exploration. Take time to answer the following questions. Consider involving your team in this process, as they might offer different perspectives.

1. Are there any specific industries or demographics that you currently serve on a regular basis? If so, what are the future opportunities like there?

2. Do you have a primary service that holds special appeal to a certain industry or demographic?

3. Are there specific industries or demographics that sound intriguing? If so, what additional research is required to determine if this track makes sense?

4. What does the competitive landscape look like for the niche you want to focus on? Is the market saturated, or is there a wide-open field?

5. What opportunities do we have to make an impact in the chosen niche? What can we do differently from everyone else?

6. Is this niche growing, flat, or declining?

7. What are you best at & passion to build or create?

Exercise

- Do some research on brands who have created the niche? See Google Trends, Similar Web, Quora, Amazon & answer the public for what people are searching & commenting.

- List down all your audiences and determine if your customers are positioning you as a niche or as generalists

- List your products, services, and target audiences, and identify potential niches you can focus on. Start creating content based on your niche

People will treat you as an authority in your field when you define your niche and they will be willing to pay what you demand, rather than dictating their own terms.

Chapter 5

Content Creation For Building Authority

Establish Your Authority in Your Field

Marketing your business with authority is about building recognition in your industry, generating online buzz, and showcasing your company's talents and skills to generate demand for your services. It is about delivering your best content and providing exceptional customer service with integrity and passion, all while actively listening to your target audience and engaging with them authentically.

In a nutshell, Authority rules. Marketing with authority is about striving for excellence in what you do and allowing that excellence to shine through. Consumers want to buy from the best and when you establish your authority in your field, you are perceived as the best.

It's about doing what YOU do best, and that's when your light begins to shine its brightest.

How to Claim Your Authority

Whatever it is that you do, it's time to step up and take ownership. If you're a marketing trainer, strive to be the best marketing trainer around. If you're a finance consultant who works with family businesses, aim to be at the top of your game, by continuously learning about trends and finding ways to address them with your clients. If you create products for hair fall protection, ensure that you produce the best hair fall protector product. If you specialize in Shopify-focused ecommerce marketing, be determined to become the best shopify ecommerce marketer.

I firmly believe that if you're going to do something, you need to do whatever it takes to do it to the best of your ability. That means continuously learning, studying your industry, reading books and trade publications, attending industry events, and enhancing your service offerings. This is a lifelong process.

Following are several ways to get you moving in the right direction. We will expand on many of these topics further in the book, but here's a primer to get you started.

Ways to build your authority
Start a Blog or create product that you are best at.
Create your own website, ecommerce website or personal brand page
Update your LinkedIn Profile page & Business Page
Update all your Social media pages
Modify the brand tagline if required
Start sharing content in social media
Join forums & groups and start talking and sharing content in those groups that helps to build your authority
Write Articles
Write a book and become a author
Make Whitepapers & Reports
Be A leader
Make videos
Get Testimonials from your clients
Start making content related to your audience & niche
Photos of awards, PR Coverage, Stage Shows

Exercise

- Don't get overwhelm with the above work
- Pick one task and implement

Chapter 6

Create Content That Converts

*"Sales Copywriting is anything intended
to persuade the right reader, viewer or
listener to take a specific action."*
~Jim Edwards

You have 3 Seconds To Get Your Message Noticed, This has reduced from 8 seconds.

From the last chapters, you achieved

1. A Marketing Mindset

2. You Identified Your Audience

3. You Identified Your Niche

Now You Will Develop Your Content That Converts

Establishing Clear Goals

Define clear objectives for your content. Are you aiming to generate leads, increase sales, or drive website traffic? Each goal requires a different approach. By setting specific and measurable goals, you can align your content strategy accordingly and track its effectiveness in converting readers into customers.

Crafting Compelling Headlines

As I said you have just 3 seconds to capture your audience attention

The headline of your content serves as the initial impression for readers. It must be attention-grabbing, compelling, and promise value. Use power words, evoke curiosity, and highlight the benefits readers will gain from engaging with your content. A strong headline enhances the chances of readers clicking through and consuming your content.

Without a strong WHY, people don't click or buy.

People will buy because they want to:

Make Money	Save Money	Save Time	Avoid Effort	Escape Mental Or Physical Pain	Get More Comfort
Achieve Greater Cleanliness	Achieve Greater Health	Gain Praise	Feel More Loved	Increase their popularity	Gain Social Status

Theme of Headlines: Customers desire, dreams, wishful thinking.

Facts: 97% of the customers don't need your product today.

If you want to become the best in your industry then you have to become the best marketer in your industry, for becoming the best you need to fulfill human needs.

Leveraging Storytelling Techniques: Storytelling is a powerful tool for creating content that converts. Craft narratives that emotionally engage readers and establish a strong connection with your brand. Utilize storytelling as a means to communicate the value of your products or services, illustrate how they solve problems, and highlight real-life success stories. By making your content relatable and memorable, you enhance the chances of converting readers into loyal customers. Look out for **My Upcoming book on detailed storytelling.**

Marketers Tell Stories….By Seth Godin

Providing Value and Solving Problems: To convert readers, your content must provide real value and address their pain points. Offer insights, tips, and actionable advice that they can implement immediately. Understand their challenges and provide practical solutions. By positioning yourself as a helpful resource, you build trust and credibility, thereby increasing the likelihood of conversion.

Incorporating Visuals: Visual content is highly effective in capturing attention and boosting engagement. Use compelling images, infographics, videos, and other visual elements to enhance your content. Visuals not only make your content more visually appealing but also improve the effectiveness of information delivery. They can showcase your products or services in action, making it easier for readers to envision themselves benefiting from what you offer. Stay tuned for…

My Upcoming Book On Compelling Visuals By Brands That Made Them Billion Dollar Brands.

Incorporating Social Proof: Leverage the power of social proof to boost conversions. Include testimonials, case studies, and reviews from satisfied customers to showcase the value and credibility of your offerings. Social proof serves as reassurance to potential customers and reduces their hesitation in making a purchase or taking the desired action. Stay tuned for…

My Upcoming Book On Detailed Analysis and Capturing Of Social Proofs.

Implementing Strong Calls-to-Action (CTAs): Having a compelling call-to-action is crucial in directing readers towards the desired conversion. Make your CTAs clear, concise, and action-oriented. Use persuasive language that motivates readers to take the next step, whether it's signing up for a newsletter, requesting a demo, or making a purchase. Place CTAs strategically throughout your content to optimize their visibility and impact.

What Will You Choose?

So, we learned, Marketing Mindset, Choosing The Audience, Owning The Nche, Building Authority & Content Creation.

Life gives 2 Paths

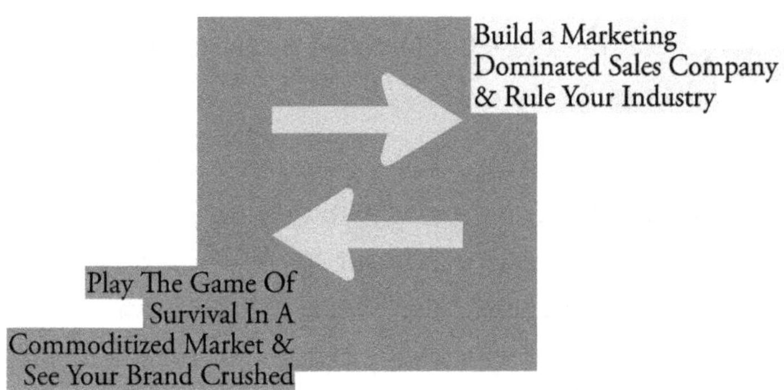

Choose The Right Person For Building The Marketing Dominated Company

Elevate Your Startup's Success with a Free 30-Minute 1-on-1 Consultation.

Are you ready to take your startup to new heights of success? Do you wish you had access to expert advice and guidance tailored specifically to your unique business challenges? Look no further! You just took the effort to be a great marketer and build a billion dollar brand by reading this book so i am excited to **offer you a rare opportunity to receive a free 30-minute one-on-one consultation** with me that is worth Rs.11,000.

I understand that the journey of building and scaling a startup can be overwhelming. That's why I want to extend a helping hand to entrepreneurs like you, offering valuable insights and strategic recommendations. My goal is to help you overcome obstacles, identify growth opportunities, and accelerate your business's progress.

During this exclusive 1-on-1 consultation, I will delve deep into your startup's specific pain points and goals. I will listen attentively to understand your vision, business model, and challenges. My aim is to identify key areas where you can optimize your operations, improve efficiency, and boost your overall performance.

Here's what you can expect from our 30-minute consultation:

1. **Personalized Guidance:** I will analyze your current situation and provide tailored recommendations to address unique needs of your startup. Whether it's refining your business strategy, optimizing your marketing efforts, or enhancing your product/service offerings. I will offer guidance specific to your requirements.

2. **Expert Insights:** I will share valuable insights, best practices, and industry trends to empower you with the knowledge you need to make informed decisions.

3. **Actionable Takeaways:** Actionable steps and a roadmap to success will be provided. I will offer you practical advice and strategies that you can implement immediately to drive tangible results in your business.

Why am I offering this free consultation? We believe in the power of collaboration and supporting the startup community. By investing my time and expertise in assisting passionate entrepreneurs like you, I aim to foster innovation, drive success, and contribute to the growth of the startup ecosystem as a whole.

Appointments for me are limited, so don't miss this opportunity to gain valuable insights that can transform your startup's trajectory. **To secure your spot, simply book the**

calendar from the link below or scan the QR Code to schedule a convenient time for your free 30-minute consultation.

https://calendly.com/meetingwithrishabh/30min

Being the reader of this book you are getting a Free 30 Minute Consulting session Worth Rs. 11000.

Remember, success favors those who seize opportunities. Let me be your trusted partner on your entrepreneurial journey, guiding you towards the achievement of your goals. We look forward to meeting you and contribute to the thriving success of your startup.

About The Author

In a world driven by relentless competition and evolving dynamics, marketing has emerged as the vital force behind every thriving business. It is no longer a luxury but a necessity, a critical component that can make or break an enterprise. And when it comes to navigating this path towards greatness, there is no one better equipped than Rishabh Gupta, a seasoned global marketing strategist with over 15 years of invaluable experience in the field of marketing and sales?

In his book, **"The Ayurveda Giant 1 Page Success Plan,"** Rishabh Gupta presents compelling strategies for Ayurveda, Skincare & FMCG startups. He firmly believes that a business without effective marketing is nothing short of a lifeless or struggling entity, incapable of meeting the demands and expectations of a fast-paced world.

Drawing upon his extensive knowledge and expertise, Rishabh shares his life mission: to empower aspiring marketers and business owners with the necessary tools and insights to excel in their craft. This book offers crisp & clear implementation strategies derived from his years of experience.

It is a roadmap to becoming a great marketer. It transcends conventional wisdom and offers a right perspective. It reminds us that true success is not solely measured by short-term gains but by the establishment of enduring connections with customers.

Whether you are a seasoned marketer looking to refine your skills or a novice eager to make a mark in the industry, Rishabh Gupta's insights will inspire and guide you towards achieving your goals. With his passion for marketing and his commitment to sharing evergreen strategies, he empowers individuals to reach new heights of success.

Prepare yourself for an exhilarating journey of discovery and transformation. "The Ayurveda Giant 1 Page Marketing Success Plan" is your key to unlocking your full potential as a marketer and carving your path to greatness. Let Rishabh Gupta be your guide as you conquer the world of marketing, one strategy at a time.

Book Summary

"The Ayurveda Giant: The 1-Page Success Marketing Plan for Ayurvedic, FMCG & Skincare Startups" is a comprehensive guide that provides valuable insights and practical strategies for entrepreneurs in the Ayurvedic, FMCG (Fast-Moving Consumer Goods), and skincare industries. Authored by Rishabh Gupta, The Global Marketing Strategist, this book serves as an essential roadmap for startups aiming to establish a strong marketing foundation and attain sustainable growth.

The book emphasizes the importance of understanding your target audience and provides detailed guidance on creating effective buyer personas. By delving into the mindset, desires, and pain points of potential customers, entrepreneurs can customize their marketing endeavors to resonate with their audience and generate meaningful engagement. The authors highlight that a well-defined buyer persona enables businesses to develop targeted marketing campaigns that deliver measurable results.

Another crucial aspect discussed in the book is the importance of specialization. Startups in these industries often encounter fierce competition, making it essential to distinguish themselves from the crowd. By focusing on a specific niche or unique selling proposition, entrepreneurs can differentiate their products and services, effectively positioning themselves as experts in their field. Rishabh provides actionable advice on identifying and capitalizing on niche markets, allowing startups to carve out a profitable and sustainable market share.

Additionally, the book offers invaluable guidance on creating compelling content that captures attention, builds trust, and converts readers into customers. It explores a range of content marketing strategies, including storytelling, educational content, user-generated content, and influencer marketing. The authors stress the importance of creating content that resonates with the values and aspirations of their target audience, fostering brand loyalty and advocacy.

In summary, "The Ayurveda Giant: The 1-Page Success Marketing Plan for Ayurvedic, FMCG & Skincare Startups" is an invaluable resource for entrepreneurs aiming to establish a solid marketing foundation. By emphasizing the importance of understanding the target audience, developing buyer personas, specializing, and creating compelling content, the book equips startups with the knowledge and tools necessary to thrive in competitive markets. Whether you are an aspiring entrepreneur or a seasoned marketer, this book provides actionable strategies and practical advice to drive success in the Ayurvedic, FMCG, and skincare industries.

Make Your <u>A-Game</u> Here

Action without vision is only passing time, vision without action is merely daydreaming, but vision with action can change the world." – Nelson Mandela

How Will You Bring Out Your Marketing Mindset?

Draft Your Detailed Audience Where You Are Able To Help Them Achieve Their Goals

Draft The Touchpoints Where Your Audience Interacts With You.

Mention what is working, What is not working & what needs to be improved?

Story Touches Heart, What's Your Story & How Your Story Will Help Your Audience?

In What Niche, Your Audience Will Treat You As An Authority & Brings You Money

How Will You Compel Your Audience To Give You Lead? (CTA, Headlines)

Do this exercise and book a slot with me for FREE AUDIT

NOTES:

NOTES:

www.ingramcontent.com/pod-product-compliance
Lightning Source LLC
LaVergne TN
LVHW011604210726

843509LV00016BA/866